The Greedy Princess
심술꾸러기 공주

The Rabbit
and the Tiger
호랑이를 골려준 토끼

HOLLYM

The Greedy Princess

A long time ago, there lived a mother with her three sons. One day she had them all sit in front of her. When they were all quiet, she told them, "We have three treasures from our ancestors. I will give one to each of you. But you must not show it to anyone."

She took out an old, worn sack that she had kept hidden away. From the sack she took out the three treasures—a big blue marble, a bamboo flute, and a patched-up vest.

심술꾸러기 공주

옛날, 어느 마을에 홀어머니와 아들 삼형제가 살고 있었습니다.

하루는 어머니가 세 아들을 불러 놓고 나직이 말했습니다.

"우리집에 옛날부터 전해 내려오는 세 가지 보물이 있단다. 너희들에게 한 가지씩 나누어 줄 테니, 누구에게도 보이지 말고 잘 간직하거라."

어머니는 허름한 자루에서 구슬 한 개와 피리 한 개, 그리고 조끼 한 벌을 꺼냈습니다.

She gave the blue marble to her oldest son, the bamboo flute to her second son, and the patched-up vest to her youngest son.

The three brothers looked at each other in disbelief.

"Mother," they all cried. "These are not treasures. They are just junk." But Mother smiled quietly. "When you roll the marble," she told her first son, "you will get a lot of money. When you blow the flute," she told her middle son, "you will be able to call a band of well-armed guards." And, she told her third son, "when you wear the vest, no one can see you."

The three brothers all winked at each other and smiled.

큰아들은 파란 구슬을 받았습니다.

둘째 아들은 낡은 피리를 받았습니다.

셋째 아들은 색이 바랜 조끼를 받았습니다.

세 아들은 고개를 갸웃거리며 어머니에게 물었습니다.

"어머니, 이건 보물이 아니잖아요?"

그러자 어머니는 조용히 웃으며 말했습니다.

"파란 구슬을 굴리면 얼마든지 돈이 나오고, 피리를 불면 날쌘 군사들이 쏟아져 나온단다. 그리고 그 조끼를 입으면 남들 눈에 보이지 않게 된단다."

세 아들은 신기한 듯이 보물을 어루만지며 좋아했습니다.

Very soon after that, Mother died.

It was not long before the first and second brothers forgot that their mother had told them not to show their treasures to anyone. They showed them to all the people in the village and bragged about their magic power.

Before long, news that the three brothers had magic treasures traveled in every direction. The news finally reached the ears of the greedy princess who lived in the great palace.

The princess said to herself, "Somehow I must get those three treasures."

The next day, the oldest brother got an invitation to visit the princess.

세 아들이 보물을 받은 지 얼마 되지 않아 어머니가 돌아가셨습니다.

그러나, 곧 큰아들과 둘째아들은 어머니가 하신 말씀을 까맣게 잊어 버리고 보물을 자랑하고 다녔습니다.

세 아들이 귀한 보물을 가지고 있다는 소문이 온 나라 안에 퍼졌습니다.

그 소문은 마침내 대궐에 사는 심술꾸러기 공주의 귀에도 들어갔습니다.

"어떻게 해서든지 세 가지 보물을 빼앗아야지."

다음날 공주는 나쁜 마음을 먹고 큰아들을 대궐로 불렀습니다.

"Oh, boy," he shouted, "I've always wanted to see the inside of the palace."

He put on his best clothes and went to the palace, taking his marble with him to show to the princess.

She entertained him in a grand manner. She showed him all around and she fed him the best food.

The young man had never seen or tasted anything like it. To impress the princess, he took the magic marble from his shirt. He rolled it. As it rolled, it left a trail of money behind.

The princess became very excited. She grabbed the marble and hid it in her dress. Then she had the young man locked in a dungeon.

"야! 나도 대궐 구경을 하게 됐다."

큰아들은 좋은 옷을 차려 입고 가슴을 두근거리며 대궐로 들어갔습니다.

공주는 큰아들에게 맛있는 음식을 내주고 대궐 구경을 시켜 주었습니다.

생전 처음 먹어 보는 음식을 대접받아 우쭐해진 큰아들은 공주를 즐겁게 해주려고 품 속에서 구슬을 꺼내어 도르르 굴렸습니다.

'좌르르르…….'

수없이 많은 돈이 쏟아져 나왔습니다.

공주는 '와' 하고 소리를 질렀습니다.

그리고는 얼른 구슬을 집어서 감추어 버렸습니다.

큰아들은 대궐 깊숙이 있는 깜깜한 광 속에 갇히고 말았습니다.

The next day she invited the second brother to visit her at the palace. She showed him all around (except the dungeon, of course) and fed him very well.

To make her happy, the second brother offered to play his magic flute for her. "When I play it, I can call a band of armed guards. They will do whatever I order," he said.

"Can I try it?"the princess asked, and grabbed the flute. She blew it at once and when the soldiers appeared, she ordered them to lock the second brother in the dungeon.

다음날, 심술꾸러기 공주는 둘째 아들을 불렀습니다.

공주는 또 맛있는 음식을 차려 놓고 둘째 아들을 구슬렀습니다.

둘째 아들은 공주를 기쁘게 해주려고 피리를 꺼냈습니다.

"공주님 제가 군사들이 나오는 피리를 불어 보겠습니다."

그러자 공주가 손을 내저으며 말렸습니다.

"내가 한빈 불어 보겠어요."

공주는 이렇게 말하고 얼른 피리를 낚아챘습니다.

그러고나서 군사들이 나오자, 둘째 아들을 광 속에 가두도록 명령하였습니다.

The third brother was very worried. His oldest brother had not returned from the palace. Neither had his other brother.

He finally put on his vest and sneaked into the palace. He crept around unnoticed and before long, he found the room of the princess. She was rolling the marble and blowing the flute and smiling very wickedly.

Unfortunately, the vest could not prevent him from sneezing. "Ah choo," he sneezed loudly.

형들이 집으로 돌아오지 않자, 막내아우는 걱정이 되었습니다.

막내아우는 보이지 않는 조끼를 입고 몰래 대궐로 숨어 들어갔습니다.

그리고 형들을 찾아 대궐 안을 샅샅이 뒤졌습니다.

막내아우는 마침내 공주의 방으로 들어갔습니다.

공주는 형들에게서 빼앗은 보물을 만지작거리며 놀고 있었습니다.

그 때 갑자기 막내아우가 '쿨럭'하고 큰 기침을 했습니다.

The princess was startled. So she hid the marble and the flute in her clothes.

The third brother waited for a while. Then he tried to ease his brother's treasures out of her dress.

He could not be seen, but he could be felt.

"A burglar!" shouted the princess. "A burglar! Help!"

She blew the bamboo flute and guards suddenly appeared.

It was all the third brother could do to get out of the room without getting caught.

Resting by the well outside the palace, he saw a tree full of delicious-looking crab apples.

공주는 깜짝 놀라서 보물을 감추었습니다.

막내아우는 보물을 빼앗으려다가 조끼자락이 나풀거리는 바람에 공주에게 들키고 말았습니다.

공주는 소스라치게 놀라며 고래고래 소리를 질렀습니다.

"도둑이야! 도둑이야!"

막내아우는 허겁지겁 도망을 쳐서 가까스로 대궐을 빠져나왔습니다.

"휴우, 하마터면 잡힐 뻔했네!"

막내아우는 터벅터벅 우물 옆을 걸어가다가 탐스럽게 열려 있는 아가위를 보았습니다.

He picked a red one and ate it. Suddenly the tip of his nose shot out away from his face.

"Oh,no!" he exclaimed. "What will I do now?" And he began to cry. As the tears dripped down his cheeks, without thinking he ate a yellow crab apple. His nose shrank and shrank, back to its normal size.

"Very strange!" he thought to himself.

Then he had an idea. He picked an armful of red crab apples and left the well.

막내아우는 빨갛게 익은 아가위를 따서 으적으적 썹어먹었습니다.

그러자, 갑자기 코가 쑥쑥 길어졌습니다.

막내아우는 깜짝 놀랐습니다.

"아니, 이걸 어떻게 하지?"

눈물을 흘리던 막내아우는 노란 아가위 한 개를 더 먹었습니다.

그랬더니 코가 스르르 짧아졌습니다.

"어, 참 이상하다. 옳지! 이걸로 공주를 혼내 줘야겠다."

막내아우는 좋은 수가 한 가지 떠올랐습니다. 그는 빨간 아가위를 한아름 땄습니다.

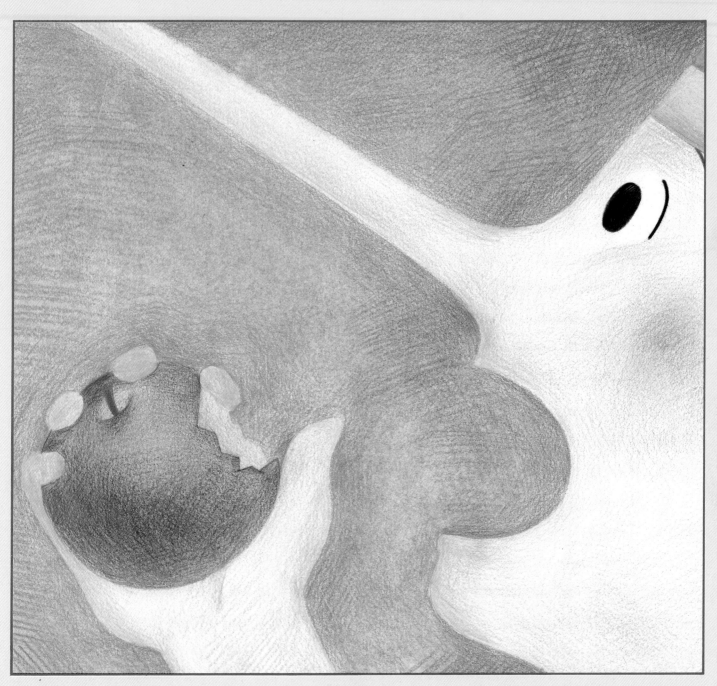

Dressing up as merchant, he went back to the palace.
"Crab apples ! Delicious crab apples !" he called.
The greedy princess came outside at once, her mouth watering.
The third brother walked up to her. He said, "Dear princess, you look very hungry. Please try one of my crab apples. I will give you one free of charge."
At the word "free," the princess grabbed up a juicy red crab apple and gobbled it up in one gulp.
Her nose shot out like an arrow.

막내아우는 아가위 장수처럼 옷을 꾸며 입고 대궐 앞으로 갔습니다.
"아가위 사려, 맛좋은 아가위 사려……."
마침 공주가 대궐 밖에 나와 있었습니다.
막내아우는 슬쩍 공주 곁으로 다가가서 아가위를 주며 말했습니다.

"공주님, 몹시 시장해 보이시는군요. 이 아가위 맛 좀 보세요. 공주님께는 거져 드리겠습니다."
욕심 많은 공주는 거져 준다는 말에 빨간 아가위를 받아들고 얼른 한 입 베어 물었습니다.
그러자 갑자기 공주의 코가 쑥쑥 길어지기 시작했습니다.

"Ow! My nose!" she shouted.

As all of the courtiers came running to see what was the matter (and to laugh at her secretly because the princess was not very well liked), the third brother crept into the palace again.

As he was wearing his vest, it did not take him long to find his brothers' treasures. But he could not find his brothers.

He blew the bamboo flute and the troop of guards appeared instantly. He ordered them to search the palace for his brothers.

Before long, all three brothers were able to leave the palace with their treasures.

They lived happily after that and kept their treasures a secret. But the greedy princess with the long ugly nose lived a long sad life.

"아이구! 내 코……."

대궐 안은 공주의 코 때문에 발칵 뒤집혔습니다.

막내아우는 얼른 보이지 않는 조끼를 입고 보물을 되찾았습니다.

막내아우는 피리를 불었습니다.

그러자 날쌘 군사들이 나와 형들을 찾아냈습니다.

막내아우와 두 형들은 궁전을 무사히 빠져 나왔습니다. 그리고 보물을 소중히 간직한 채, 행복하게 살았습니다.

그러나 심술꾸러기 공주는 길게 늘어진 코를 달고 눈물을 흘리며 살았습니다.

The Rabbit and the Tiger

One sunny spring day, Rabbit was just waking up from a very pleasant, peaceful nap in the shade of a big rock.

"Ummm," he said as he stretched. "I slept well."

And then, just as he stood up he heard a loud noise. Frightened, he looked around and saw a huge tiger just a few feet away.

호랑이를 골려 준 토끼

따스한 햇볕이 내리쬐는 봄날, 토끼 한 마리가 바위 밑에서 쿨쿨 낮잠을 자고 있었습니다.

"아함, 잘 잤다."

늘어지게 낮잠을 자고 난 토끼는 기지개를 켜며 일어났습니다.

그런데 갑자기 '으르렁' 하는 큰 소리가 났습니다.

깜짝 놀란 토끼가 고개를 들어보니 커다란 호랑이 한 마리가 떡 버티고 있는 것이었습니다.

"How nice to meet you here, Rabbit," said Tiger. "Since I'm very hungry, I think I will swallow you at once."

Tiger moved his watery mouth close to Rabbit.

"How nice to meet you here, Tiger," said Rabbit, who was very worried and thinking hard. "But don't eat me right away. Wait just a moment."

"Why?" growled Tiger.

"Wouldn't you like some rice cakes first? I know you are very hungry and I am too small to make a good meal for such a big tiger," Rabbit explained.

"Is this some kind of trick?" asked Tiger.

"How could you even think such a thing?" Rabbit replied.

"어흥, 배가 고프던 참에 잘 됐다. 너를 잡아 먹어야겠다."

호랑이는 입맛을 쩍쩍 다시며 토끼에게 다가왔습니다.

"아이구, 호랑이 아저씨! 잠깐만 기다려 주세요."

토끼는 얼른 한 가지 꾀를 생각해 냈습니다.

"아저씨, 나같은 건 나중에 잡아먹고 우선 맛있는 떡이나 먹어 보는 게 어때요?"

"뭐라고? 네놈이 날 속이려는 거지."

"호랑이 아저씨, 누구 앞이라고 제가 거짓말을 하겠어요."

"All right then," purred Tiger. "Give me the rice cakes before I eat you. And be quick about it."

"It will only take me a second to get the rice cakes. I have some just on the other side of this rock." Rabbit hopped, hopped to the other side and picked up eleven smooth white stones.

Then he hopped, hopped back to Tiger, who was very dubious.

"These look like stones." growled Tiger, showing his teeth.

"Silly beast," Rabbit said, "rice cakes always look like stones until you cook them. Just wait, You'll see."

Then Rabbit hopped, hopped around, picking up sticks to make a fire. When he had a nice blaze going, he put the rocks in it.

"그래, 그렇다면 얼른 그 떡을 내봐 봐라."

호랑이는 군침을 삼키며 말했습니다.

"아저씨, 제가 얼른 가져올 테니 잠깐만 기다리세요."

토끼는 깡총깡총 바위 뒤로 뛰어가 돌멩이 열한 개를 주워왔습니다.

그리고 호랑이 앞에 돌멩이 열한 개를 좍 늘어 놓았습니다.

"아니, 이건 돌멩이 아니냐?"

"아저씨도 참, 불에 구워야 제 맛이 나는 군떡도 모르세요?"

토끼는 이렇게 말하고 나서 마른 나뭇가지를 주워모아 불을 지피고, 그 위에 돌멩이를 올려 놓았습니다.

As the stones got hotter and hotter, he chatted with Tiger about the weather and so on as though they were close friends and soon Tiger no longer doubted him.

"Oh, oh," Rabbit said. "I forgot to get the soy sauce."

"Soy sauce?" queried Tiger. "What is that?"

"Don't you know?" Rabbit teased. "It makes cooked rice cakes taste much better. I will get some and be right back. But while I'm gone you have to watch the rice cakes so they don't burn."

"All right, all right. Don't take all day," Tiger growled.

돌은 점점 더 뜨거워졌습니다.

토끼와 호랑이는 오랜 친구처럼 여러 이야기를 나누었습니다. 호랑이는 더 이상 토끼를 의심하지 않게 되었습니다.

그 때 토끼가

"아참"

하고 소리를 쳤습니다.

"내가 간장을 깜빡 잊었네!"

"간장? 간장이란 게 뭐냐?"

"아저씬 그것도 모르세요? 이 군떡은 간장을 찍어 먹어야 더 맛있어요. 제가 아랫마을에 가서 간장을 얻어 올 테니, 떡이나 타지 않게 잘 보고 계세요."

"그래, 빨리 갔다 오너라."

As Rabbit hopped, hopped away as quickly as he could, he looked back over his shoulder. "I'll be right back, Tiger," he called. "But promise me you won't eat any of those ten rice cakes until I return. Okay?" And he hopped, hopped away, laughing all the time.

Tiger sat and sat in front of the fire, getting hungrier and hungrier. The stones got redder and redder.

As Tiger waited, he counted the 'rice cakes' in the fire.

"One. Two. Three. Four. Five. Six. Seven. Eight. Nine. Ten. Eleven."

호랑이가 이렇게 외치자. 토끼가 뒤를 돌아보며 큰 소리로 말했습니다.

"아저씨, 떡이 모두 열 개니까. 제가 올 때까지 한 개도 먹으면 안 돼요."

그러고나서 토끼는 쏜살같이 산등성이를 넘어갔습니다.

호랑이는 불 옆에 쭈그리고 앉아 떡이 구워질 때만 기다리고 있었습니다.

"군떡아, 군떡아, 빨리빨리 익어라. 군떡 하나, 군떡 둘, 군떡 셋……. 어? 이상하다."

떡을 세어 보던 호랑이는 고개를 갸웃거렸습니다.

"Eleven?" Tiger counted again. "Eleven! That silly Rabbit. Well, I'll eat just one rice cake before he comes back. He'll never know the difference."

So without waiting a moment longer, Tiger ate one of the red-hot stones.

"Hot! It's hot! It's too hot!" Tiger screamed and jumped and ran as the stone burned his mouth, his throat, his stomach. "Hot! Hot! Hot!"

군떡은 아무리 세어 봐도 열한 개였습니다.

"바보같은 토끼녀석, 열한 개의 떡을 보고 열 개라고? 하하, 나머지 한 개는 몰래 먹어치워야지."

배고픈 호랑이는 불에 올려놓은 돌멩이 중에서 가장 큰 것을 골라 한입에 꿀꺽 삼켜 버렸습니다.

"앗 뜨거! 앗 뜨거!"

호랑이는 이리저리 펄쩍펄쩍 뛰었습니다.

"아이구 배야. 아이구 배야."

빨갛게 단 돌멩이를 집어삼킨 호랑이는 배를 움켜쥐고 떼굴떼굴 굴렀습니다.

Because of his burns, Tiger could not eat anything for many days. He just stayed in bed and thought about what Rabbit had done to him.

When he was well enough to leave his cave, Tiger was terribly hungry and terribly angry.

While he was looking for something to eat, he chanced to bump into Rabbit again.

"How pleasant to meet you again," Tiger growled. "Did you think you could get away with that bad trick you played on me?" he said and opened his mouth to eat Rabbit.

Rabbit smiled and thought quickly. "Why are you mad at me? But maybe there was some sort of misunderstanding."

입 안을 온통 덴 호랑이는 아무것도 먹지 못하고 며칠 동안 끙끙 앓았습니다.

"아이고 배고파라."

굴 속에서 한참을 지낸 호랑이는 어슬렁어슬렁 굴 밖으로 기어나왔습니다.

먹을 것을 찾아다니던 호랑이는 깡총깡총 뛰어오는 토끼를 만났습니다.

"네 이놈, 잘 만났다! 날 그렇게 골탕먹이고도 살아 남을 줄 알았느냐?"

호랑이는 두 눈을 부릅뜨고 으르렁거렸습니다.

"제가 왜 아저씨를 화나게 하겠어요? 뭔가 오해하고 계시는군요?"

Tiger did not know what to say.

"I have an idea!" Rabbit said.

"Oh, no. Not again," Tiger growled. "I won't let you trick me again."

"Trick? Oh, no, of course not," Rabbit answered him. "In fact, I was just on my way to your cave. I wanted to tell you how to catch birds just by opening your mouth."

Tiger was very hungry. Just thinking about eating birds made his mouth water more and more.

호랑이는 말문이 막혔습니다.

"아저씨 화만 내지 말고, 제 말 좀 들어 보세요."

토끼는 다시 한번 꾀를 내어 말했습니다.

"이 나쁜 녀석아, 내가 또 속아넘어 갈 줄 아느냐?"

호랑이는 토끼를 잡아먹을 듯이 바싹 다가왔습니다.

"아저씨! 잠깐만 참으세요. 전 지금 아저씨를 만나러 가는 길이었어요. 호랑이 아저씨를 위해서 가만히 입만 벌리고 있어도 참새를 잡을 수 있는 방법을 생각해 냈단 말이에요."

배가 너무나 고팠던 호랑이는 토끼의 거짓말에 또 귀가 솔깃해졌습니다.

"Are you sure this isn't a trick?" Tiger asked.

"Of course not," Rabbit reassured him. "Just trust me."

Rabbit led Tiger into the middle of a field of weeds. Rabbit told Tiger to open his mouth as wide as he could while Rabbit chased the birds toward him. Then Rabbit hopped, hopped away.

So Tiger waited as patiently as he could, with his head up and his mouth open. To pass the time, he closed his eyes and thought about how good the birds would taste.

Far away, he could hear Rabbit making noise. "Shoo, shoo," he heard Rabbit say.

He also heard a sound that crackled and sizzled, but he did not pay much attention to it.

"그게 정말이냐?"

호랑이는 군침을 삼키며 물었습니다.

"정말이고말고요. 저를 따라오세요."

토끼는 호랑이를 억새밭 가운데로 끌고 갔습니다.

"아저씨, 여기서 입을 크게 벌리고 계세요. 저는 저 쪽에 가서 참새떼를 몰겠어요."

호랑이는 입을 딱 벌리고 앉아 참새떼를 기다렸습니다.

호랑이는 눈을 감고 새고기가 얼마나 맛좋을까 생각해 보았습니다.

멀리서 '후여후여' 하고 참새떼를 쫓는 토끼의 목소리가 들려왔습니다.

그리고 곧 '버적버적' 하는 소리가 났습니다.

41

The crackling sound became louder and louder. Tiger thought the crackling was the twittering of birds. He thought, "Oh, boy, the noise is getting louder and louder. The birds must be getting closer and closer."

He became even more excited and he opened his mouth even wider.

It got hotter and hotter. Tiger finally opened his eyes and saw the weed field burning all around him. Rabbit had set it afire.

"Hot! It's hot! It's too hot! Hot! Hot! Hot!" yelped Tiger as he ran from the field.

버적거리는 소리는 점점 더 크게 들렸습니다.

"참새떼가 무척 많은가 보다."

호랑이는 신이 나서 입을 더 크게 벌렸습니다.

그런데 갑자기 볼기짝이 후끈거렸습니다.

깜짝 놀란 호랑이가 뒤를 돌아보니, 억새밭은 온통 불바다가 되어 활활 타고 있었습니다.

토끼가 불을 지른 것입니다.

"앗 뜨거! 앗 뜨거!"

호랑이는 허겁지겁 억새밭을 뛰어나왔습니다.

"Oh, no. Rabbit tricked me again.
This time I'm lucky to be alive."
The hungry tiger was so badly burned that he
had to spend many painful days in his cave.
But he had plenty to think about.

"아이구, 내가 토끼한테 또 속았구나."
온몸을 불에 덴 호랑이는 아무것도
먹지 못하고 또다시 굴 속에서
끙끙 앓았습니다.